D0961232

Houndsley
and
Catina
Plink and Plunk

Houndsley
and
Catina
Plink and Plunk

James Howe

illustrated by Marie-Louise Gay

CANDLEWICK PRESS

for Nathan and Kendra Lee
J. H.

Text copyright © 2009 by James Howe
Illustrations copyright © 2009 by Marie-Louise Gay

First edition 2009

Library of Congress Cataloging-in-Publication Data

Howe, James, date.
Houndsley and Catina plink and plunk / by James Howe ;
illustrated by Marie Louise Gay. — 1st ed.
p.   cm.
Summary: Houndsley likes canoeing and his friend Catina likes bicycling,
but each has to help the other learn to enjoy these activities in order to do them together.
ISBN 978-0-7636-3385-1
[1. Canoes and canoeing—Fiction. 2. Bicycles and bicycling—Fiction. 3. Friendship—
Fiction. 4. Dogs—Fiction. 5. Cats—Fiction.]   I. Gay, Marie-Louise, ill. II. Title.
PZ7.H83727Houp 2009
[E]—dc22   2007032002

2 4 6 8 10 9 7 5 3 1

Printed in China

This book was typeset in Galliard and Tree-Boxelder.
The illustrations were done in watercolor, pencil, and collage.

Candlewick Press
99 Dover Street
Somerville, Massachusetts 02144

visit us at www.candlewick.com

Contents

Chapter One
Plink

Houndsley loved to canoe.

Each spring he waited for the first

warm day to take his canoe out on the lake.

His friend Bert usually went with him.

But this year Bert could not go.

"My aunt is in the hospital," said Bert. "I am going to visit her."

"You are a good nephew," Houndsley replied. "I will give you some vegetable soup to take with you."

"Does it have worms?" Bert asked. "Aunt Martha is fond of worms."

"It does not," said Houndsley. "But I could put some noodles in it."

"Noodles are almost as good as worms,"
Bert said. "Thank you, Houndsley."

After Bert left, Houndsley wondered who else he might ask to go canoeing with him. He could invite his best friend, Catina. He liked doing everything with Catina. Everything, that is, but canoeing.

For some reason, whenever they went canoeing, Catina talked the entire time. She did not seem to understand that for Houndsley the joys of canoeing were the boat's silent glide over the water, the *plink* and *plunk* of the paddles, the calling of the birds as they swooped overhead, the rustle of the wind in the pines at the water's edge.

Perhaps, thought Houndsley, *this time will be different.*

It was not. From the moment Catina
set foot in the canoe, she talked. And
talked. And talked.

Did you hear about...

Houndsley, wha

Did yo

Houndsley could not hear the birds or the *plink* and *plunk* of the paddles. All he could hear was Catina's voice. *I wish she would stop talking,* Houndsley thought.

Suddenly, the canoe was caught in the wake of a passing boat. Up and down it went in the wavy water.

"Oh!" Catina cried.

"Hold on!" cried Houndsley.

16

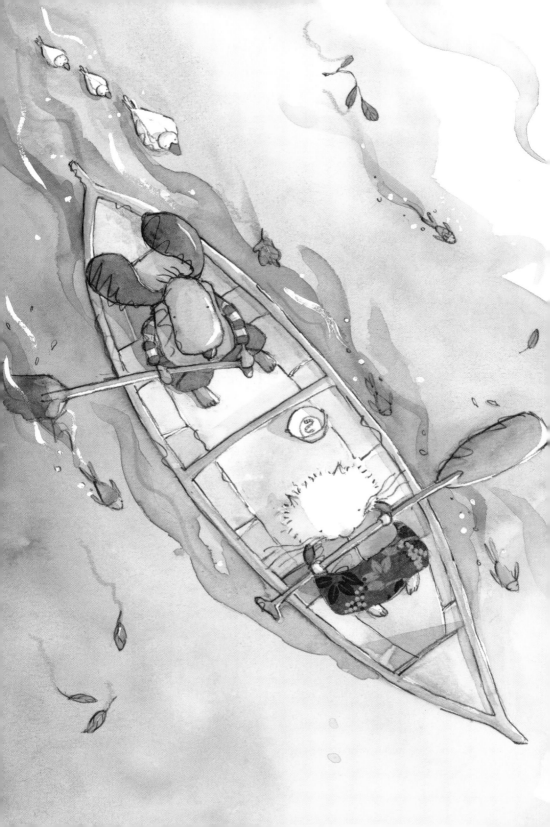

Catina gripped her paddle and clamped her eyes shut.

"Are you all right?" Houndsley called out to Catina when the water settled down.

Catina nodded her head but did not say a word.

At last Houndsley could enjoy the peace and quiet he wanted. But now that his wish had been granted, he began to worry. *What is wrong with Catina?* he thought. *Why has she stopped talking?*

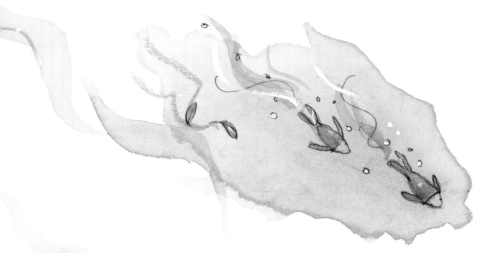

Chapter Two
Crash!

One morning Houndsley was working in

his garden when he heard a *honk*. Mimi was

delivering the mail.

"I have a package for you!" Mimi

called out. "It's so big that I will need

your help."

Just then, Catina came by on her
bicycle.

"What is it?" Catina asked.

"I don't know," said Houndsley. "It's
a surprise." He opened the envelope that
was on the outside of the box and read the
note inside:

Dear Cousin Houndsley,
   I was doing my spring
cleaning and found this.
I don't use it anymore. I seem
to remember that you do not
have one. Now you do!
Have fun!
   Love,
      Cousin Wagster

"A bicycle!" Catina cried out when the box had been opened.

Houndsley didn't say anything. He thought of the bicycle he had just given away in his own spring cleaning. Cousin Wagster had forgotten that Houndsley owned a bicycle because Houndsley had never ridden it.

"Biking is one of my favorite things to do," Catina exclaimed. "We have never done it together, Houndsley. Why is that?"

Before Houndsley could answer, she went on, "Well, there is no time like the present. Let's go for a ride!"

Houndsley looked down at his feet. "Perhaps we could go next week," he said to Catina. "I have to plant my garden and . . . and . . ."

"You can plant your garden this afternoon," Catina said. "I will help you."

"It might rain," Houndsley said, his soft-as-a-rose-petal voice growing softer with each word.

"There is not a cloud in the sky," Catina replied. "Mimi, would you like to go with us?"

"I have more mail to deliver," said

Mimi. "But thank you for asking."

"I'll go with you," said a new voice.

No one had seen Bert arrive from his house

20

next door. "I'll get my bicycle—well, it is really a tricycle—and be right back!"

Oh, dear, thought Houndsley. *I do not want to go for a ride. But how do I say no?*

A few minutes later, the three friends set off. Catina led the way, followed by Bert, and slowly, slowly by Houndsley.

Houndsley wibbled. Houndsley wobbled.

Houndsley's feet flew up in the air.

Crash!

Houndsley landed in a cluster of azalea bushes. He held on to his helmet while his upside-down bicycle wheels went spinning.

"Are you all right?" Catina cried.

Houndsley nodded.

"Houndsley," said Bert, "do you not know how to ride a bicycle?"

Feeling his face grow hot, Houndsley said in almost a whisper, "How did you guess?"

Bert began to laugh. Catina laughed, too. And soon Houndsley was laughing so hard, tears came to his eyes.

"Let's trade," said Bert when they were done laughing. "You can begin with three wheels, and before you know it, you will be ready for two!"

Chapter Three
Plunk

Houndsley packed a picnic lunch, and the three friends went for a long bicycle ride. He felt much safer on Bert's tricycle, and it wasn't long before he was willing to try his own two-wheeler again.

"You're doing it!" Bert cried as Houndsley pedaled down a country lane.

Houndsley wibbled. And Houndsley wobbled. But Houndsley stayed out of the azalea bushes and even stopped the bike by himself without falling over.

"Hooray for Houndsley!" Catina and Bert shouted.

As they spread their lunch on the blanket Houndsley had packed, Catina said, "There is something I must tell you, Houndsley. Do you remember how I talked so much when we went for our canoe ride?"

Houndsley did not want to hurt his friend's feelings, so he said, "Hmm, I'm not sure I do. But I remember how quiet you got after we almost tipped over."

"Yes," said Catina. "I got quiet because I was scared. And I was talking for the same reason. I talk a lot when I'm nervous."

"But what makes you nervous about canoeing?" Houndsley asked.

"I...I don't like water," Catina admitted. "I do not know how to swim."

"But you have gone canoeing with me many times," said Houndsley. "And have you been nervous every time?"

Catina nodded.

Bert passed her a pickle.

"That does not sound like fun," said Houndsley. "I am sorry you didn't tell me."

"I didn't want you to feel bad. You are my friend, and I wanted to do what you wanted to do."

Houndsley understood. "That is why I agreed to go biking, even though I was nervous."

"But then we taught you how to ride," said Bert. "So now you don't have to be nervous anymore."

"And I will teach you how to swim," Houndsley told Catina. "We will go to the lake tomorrow. Can you come with us, Bert?"

"Yes," said Bert. "My aunt is out of the hospital. I think it was your vegetable soup that made her better. She said those were the best worms she ever had. I did not tell her they were noodles."

The next day, Houndsley, Catina, and Bert went to the lake.

"You are very good at the dog paddle," Houndsley told Catina.

"Thank you," said Catina.

Soon the three friends took the canoe out on the water. Their paddles *plink*ed and *plunk*ed. The birds called as they swooped overhead. The wind rustled in the pines at the water's edge.

No one said a word. Not even Catina.